Rip Van Winkle

For my wife Loretta,
daughter Yvette,
and son Justin
—D.S.S.

Rip Van Winkle

Retold by **Morrell Gipson**

Based on the story by Washington Irving

Illustrated by **Daniel San Souci**

DOUBLEDAY & COMPANY, INC. ● GARDEN CITY, NEW YORK

Library of Congress Catalog Card Number 83-20624
ISBN: 0-385-18757-2 Trade   0-385-18758-0 Prebound   0-385-23965-3 (pbk.)
Text copyright © 1984 by Doubleday & Company, Inc. Illustrations copyright © 1984 by Daniel San Souci
All Rights Reserved   Printed in the United States of America
Designed by Judith Neuman
Library of Congress Cataloging in Publication Data
Gipson, Morrell
  Rip Van Winkle.
  Summary: A man who sleeps for twenty years in the Catskill Mountains wakes to a much-changed world.
  [1. Catskill Mountains region (N.Y.)—Fiction.
2. New York (State)—Fiction] I. San Souci, Daniel, ill.
II. Irving, Washington. Rip Van Winkle. III. Title.
PZ7.G4394Ri 1984   [Fic]   9 8 7 6 5 4 3   (hc)   9 8 7 6 5 4 3 2 1 (pbk.)

Anyone who has made a voyage up the Hudson River has seen the great Catskill Mountains away to the west, swelling up to a noble height. Long, long ago the Indians believed the mountains were enchanted, inhabited by spirits who controlled the weather—spreading sunshine or clouds, and sending good or bad hunting seasons. Later, when the first Dutch settlers came, they, too, thought the mountains were haunted.

Our story begins in a little village that nestled at the very foot of these mountains, at a time when the country still belonged to Great Britain and was ruled by King George III. There lived in this village a simple, good-natured fellow named Rip Van Winkle, who was loved by everyone—except his wife.

Rip was always willing to lend his neighbors a helping hand. He was the best man around for husking corn or building stone fences. And for the housewives, he did the errands and odd jobs that their husbands refused.

The children shouted with joy whenever Rip approached. He helped them at their sports, made their playthings, taught them to fly kites and shoot marbles, and told them stories of ghosts, witches, and Indians. Wherever Rip went in the village he was surrounded by a troop of young ones hanging on his coattail, clambering on his back, and playing a thousand tricks on him. And there was not a dog in the village that would bark at him.

The trouble was that Rip Van Winkle was ready to attend to anybody's business but his own. Dame Van Winkle was always scolding him about his idleness, his carelessness, and the ruin he was bringing on his family. Morning, noon, and night she lectured him. Rip would shrug his shoulders, shake his head, cast up his eyes, and say nothing, which made his wife even angrier. Finally Rip and his dog Wolf would take to the outside of the house—the only side that, in truth, belongs to a henpecked husband.

He would fish all day without a murmur, even if he didn't get a single bite. He would trudge through woods and swamps for hours with his heavy gun on his shoulder, to hunt squirrels or wild pigeons. But he declared it was of no use to work on his farm. It was the worst piece of ground in the whole country, he said; everything about it went wrong, and would go wrong, in spite of him. His fences were always falling to pieces; his cow would go astray or get into the cabbages; weeds grew more quickly in his fields than anywhere else. Little by little, Rip's land had dwindled away until he had only a patch of corn and potatoes, and it was still the worst-kept farm in the neighborhood.

His children, too, were as ragged and wild, as if they belonged to nobody. Young Rip had inherited the habits as well as the old clothes of his father, and was generally seen trooping around in a pair of tattered trousers that he had to hold up with one hand.

Times got worse and worse for Rip as the years rolled on and Dame Van Winkle's tongue grew sharper with constant use. Whenever he was driven from home, he sought refuge with friends who sat all day long on a bench in front of the village inn. There they talked over village gossip or told endless stories about nothing. Sometimes they listened to an old newspaper that a traveler had left behind, read aloud by the schoolmaster, Derrick Van Bummel, who could pronounce the largest words without a stammer.

This group of philosophers was presided over by Nicholas Vedder, the landlord of the inn. He was never heard to speak, but when anything displeased him he would smoke his pipe with short, angry puffs. And when he agreed with a remark, he sent long, lazy smoke rings into the air.

Alas, the unlucky Rip was even routed from this stronghold by his angry wife, who broke in upon the tranquil group to rage against all the members. She even accused Nicholas Vedder himself of encouraging her husband in habits of idleness.

Rip was almost reduced to despair. Now his only escape from the labor of the farm and the clamor of his wife was to take his gun and his faithful Wolf and wander away into the woods.

After a long ramble of this kind on a fine autumn day, Rip stopped to rest in one of the highest parts of the Catskill Mountains. On one side below him he could see miles and miles of rich woodland, with the mighty Hudson River in the distance. On the other side he looked down into a deep mountain glen—wild, lonely, dark, and filled with rocks from the cliffs around.

For some time he lay enjoying the scene, but the mountains began to throw their long blue shadows over the valleys, and he saw that it would be dark before he reached the village. Sighing at the thought of encountering the terrors of his wife, he was about to descend when he heard a voice in the distance hallooing, "Rip Van Winkle! Rip Van Winkle!"

Rip looked around and saw nothing but a crow winging its solitary flight across the mountains. He thought, "I must have imagined it," and turned again to leave, when he heard the same cry ring through the still evening air: "Rip Van Winkle! Rip Van Winkle!"

Wolf bristled, growled, and skulked to his master's side. Rip himself began to feel frightened, and he looked anxiously down into the glen. He saw a strange figure slowly toiling up the rocks, bending under the weight of something he carried on his back.

Rip was surprised to see anyone in this lonely place, but he thought it might be one of his neighbors in need of help, and he hastened down.

As he approached, he was still more amazed at the stranger's appearance. He was a short, square-built old fellow with thick bushy hair and a grizzled beard. His dress was of the antique Dutch fashion of earlier years. On his shoulders he bore a stout keg that seemed full of liquor, and he made signs for Rip to help him with the load.

Although Rip felt shy and distrustful of the stranger, he complied with his usual good nature. Taking turns with the keg, they clambered up a narrow gully. As they climbed, Rip every now and then heard long, rolling peals like distant thunder. The noise seemed to come out of a deep cleft between lofty rocks, toward which they were heading.

Now, this whole time Rip and his companion had labored on in silence. Although Rip marveled greatly as to the purpose of carrying a keg of liquor up the wild mountains, there was something about the stranger that made him hold his tongue.

Passing through the cleft in the rocks, they came to a hollow surrounded by steep cliffs. And there Rip beheld a wondrous scene: In the middle of the hollow, a company of odd-looking men were playing at ninepins. They were all dressed in the quaint fashion of Rip's guide. There was one who seemed to be the leader. He was a stout old

gentleman with a weather-beaten face; and he wore a high-crowned hat
and feather, red stockings, and high-heeled shoes with roses on them.

The group reminded Rip of the figures in an old painting in the parlor
of the village parson, which the earliest settlers had brought over from
Holland. It seemed especially odd to him that even though these folks
were playing a game, they were solemn and silent. They were the most
melancholy party of pleasure he had ever seen. Nothing interrupted the
stillness but the noise of the rolling balls, which echoed along the
mountains like peals of thunder.

As Rip and his companion approached the group, they suddenly stopped playing and stared at him with such strange, pale faces that Rip's heart turned within him and his knees knocked together. His companion now emptied the keg into large flagons and made signs to Rip to serve the company. Rip obeyed in fear and trembling. The players drank the liquor in profound silence and went back to their game.

By degrees, Rip's fear and anxiety subsided. He even ventured, when no one was looking, to sample the beverage, which he found excellent. One taste provoked another; and he went back to the flagon so often that at length his eyes swam, his head nodded, and he fell into a deep sleep.

When Rip woke up, he found himself on the green knoll from which he had first seen the old man of the glen. He rubbed his eyes. It was a bright, sunny morning. "Surely I have not slept here all night!" he said. "Oh, that wicked flagon! What excuse shall I make to Dame Van Winkle?"

He looked around for his gun, but instead of his clean, well-oiled fowling piece he found an old, rusty firelock. He whistled and shouted for Wolf, but the dog had disappeared. Now he suspected that the silent men of the night before had tricked and robbed him.

Rip decided to revisit the scene of the last evening, to demand his dog and gun. As he got up, he found himself stiff in the joints. "These mountain beds do not agree with me," he thought. "If this frolic should lay me up with a fit of rheumatism, I shall have a blessed time with Dame Van Winkle."

With some difficulty he climbed down into the glen. He found the gully he and his companion had climbed, but to his astonishment a mountain stream was now foaming down it. Somehow he scrambled up the sides, and he finally reached the place where the opening led through the cliffs to the hollow. But no trace of such an opening remained. The rocks were a high, impenetrable wall, over which the water tumbled in a sheet of feathery foam.

Poor Rip could go no farther. He whistled and called again for his dog but was answered only by the cawing of a flock of idle crows. He was famished for his breakfast. He grieved to give up his dog and gun; he dreaded to meet his wife; but it would not do to starve among the mountains. He shook his head, shouldered the rusty firelock, and with a troubled heart turned his footsteps homeward.

As Rip approached his village, he met a number of people, none of whom he knew. This surprised him. Their dress, too, was different from that to which he was accustomed. They all stared at him with equal surprise, and whenever they did they stroked their chins. Rip found himself doing the same, and to his astonishment he felt a beard that had grown a foot long!

He entered the village, and a troop of strange children ran at his heels, hooting and pointing at his gray beard. The dogs, too, barked as he passed—and he recognized not one of them.

The village itself was changed. It was much larger, and there were rows of houses he had never seen before. Strange names were over the doors, and strange faces were at the windows. Everything was so different that his mind now misgave him, and he began to think that both he and the world about him were bewitched. Surely this was his native village, which he had left the day before. There stood the Catskill Mountains; there ran the silver Hudson; there were every hill and dale precisely as they had always been. Rip was sorely perplexed. "That drink last night," he thought, "has addled my poor head sadly!"

At last he found his way to his own house, which he approached with dread, expecting every moment to hear the shrill voice of Dame Van Winkle. He found his home gone to decay—the roof fallen in, the windows shattered, and the doors off the hinges. A half-starved dog that looked like Wolf was skulking around and Rip called him by name, but the cur showed his teeth and passed on. This was the unkindest cut of all. "My very dog," sighed poor Rip, "has forgotten me!"

He entered the house, which Dame Van Winkle had always kept in neat order. It was empty and forlorn. He called loudly for his wife and children. The lonely rooms rang for a moment with his voice, and then all again was silence.

Now Rip hastened to his old refuge, the village inn. But it, too, was gone. In its place stood a large, rickety, wooden building, and over the door was painted "The Union Hotel, by Jonathan Doolittle." Instead of the great tree that had sheltered the little Dutch inn, there was a tall, naked pole from which fluttered a flag Rip had never seen before, with a strange design of stars and stripes.

A crowd of people were around the door, but he knew none of them. They were busy, bustling, arguing; it was quite unlike the drowsy tranquillity Rip had expected. A long, lean fellow with his pockets full of handbills was speaking about rights of citizens—elections—members of Congress—liberty—heroes of seventy-six—and other words that meant nothing at all to the bewildered Rip Van Winkle.

With his long, grizzled beard, rusty gun, and ragged dress, Rip soon attracted everyone's attention. The speaker hurried up to him and inquired on which side he would vote. Rip stared at him in silence. Another fellow whispered in his ear to ask whether he was Federal or Democrat. Rip was at a loss to understand the questions. Then a well-dressed old gentleman planted himself before Rip and asked, "What brings you to the election with a gun on your shoulders and a mob at your heels? Do you mean to breed a riot in the village?"

"Alas, sir!" cried Rip. "I am a poor, quiet man, a native of the place, and a loyal subject of the King, God bless him!"

A shout burst from the crowd: "A tory! A tory! A spy! Away with him!"

The self-important old gentleman managed to restore order. Then he asked Rip again why he had come there, and whom he was seeking. Poor Rip humbly assured him that he meant no harm—he was merely looking for his friends who used to be around the tavern.

"Well, who are they? Name them."

Rip asked, "Where is Nicholas Vedder?"

There was silence until an old man piped up in a quavering voice, "Why, Nicholas Vedder is dead and gone these eighteen years!"

"Where is Van Bummel, the schoolmaster?"

"He went off to the war, became a great general, and he's now in Congress."

Rip's heart sank as he heard of these sad changes and found himself alone in a world that he did not understand. He cried out in despair, "Does nobody here know Rip Van Winkle?"

"Why, there is Rip Van Winkle," exclaimed two or three. "To be sure, there he is leaning against the tree."

Rip looked, and he beheld an exact likeness of himself as he had gone up the mountain. "I'm not myself," Rip exclaimed. "I'm somebody else. That's me yonder—no, that was myself last night. But I fell asleep on the mountain, and they changed my gun, and everything's changed, and I'm changed, and I can't tell my name or who I am!"

The people looked at each other, nodded and winked, and tapped their foreheads. At this moment a young woman with a child in her arms pressed through the crowd to get a look. The child was frightened by Rip and began to cry. "Hush, Rip," she cried. "The old man won't hurt you."

The name of the child, the air of the mother, and the tone of her voice, awakened a train of memories in Rip's mind. "What's your name, my good woman?" he asked.

"Judith Gardenier."

"And your father's name?"

"Ah, poor man, Rip Van Winkle was his name. But it's been twenty years since he went away, and has never been heard of since. His dog came home without him. I was then but a little girl."

Rip had one more question. He put it with a shaking voice. "Where's your mother?"

"Oh, she died a short time ago. She broke a blood vessel in a fit of anger at a New England peddler."

Rip could contain himself no longer. He caught his daughter and her child in his arms. "I am your father," he cried. "Young Rip Van Winkle once, old Rip Van Winkle now. Does nobody know poor Rip Van Winkle?"

All stood amazed, until an old woman tottered out from the crowd and peered into his face. "Sure enough, it is Rip Van Winkle himself! Welcome home, old neighbor! Where have you been these twenty long years?"

Rip's story was soon told, for the whole twenty years had been to him as one night. The neighbors stared when they heard it, and winked at each other, and put their tongues in their cheeks.

Then old Peter Vanderdonk was seen slowly coming down the road. Peter was the oldest inhabitant of the village and well versed in all its history and traditions. He remembered Rip at once. And he assured the company that it was a fact, handed down from his ancestors, that the Catskill Mountains had always been haunted by strange beings. It was believed, he told them, that the great Hendrick Hudson, who had discovered the river and its surroundings, kept a kind of vigil there every twenty years—along with the crew of his ship, the *Half Moon*. Moreover, Peter said, his own father had seen Captain Hudson and his men in their old Dutch dresses playing at ninepins in a hollow of the mountains. And he himself had heard one summer afternoon the sound of their balls, like distant peals of thunder.

To make a long story short, the company broke up and returned to their election arguments. Rip's daughter took him home to live in her snug house. She had a stout, cheery farmer for a husband, whom Rip remembered as one of the urchins who used to climb upon his back. Rip's son, who had been seen leaning against the tree, was employed to work on the farm, but he showed an inherited disposition to attend to anything else but his own business.

Rip had arrived at that happy age when a man can be idle without criticism. He took his place once more on the bench at the inn door; and he was looked upon as one of the wise old men of the village. It was some time before he could keep straight the strange events that had taken place during his sleep: that the country had thrown off the yoke of old England, and that instead of being a subject of His Majesty George III, he was now a free citizen of the United States.

He used to tell his story to every stranger who arrived at Mr. Doolittle's hotel. At first the tale varied on some points every time he told it, but at last it settled down precisely to the one related here. And every man, woman, and child in the neighborhood knew it by heart!